ROSIE'S FAMILY
An adoption story

By Lori Rosove
Pictures by Heather Burrill

Published by Asia Press
Ontario, Canada

A special thanks to Heather Burrill for ingeniously bringing *Rosie* "to life" and to Susana Zedic for her brilliant technical contribution and her unbound enthusiasm.

Canadian Cataloguing in Publication Data

Rosove, Lori, 1963-
    Rosie's family : an adoption story

ISBN   978-0-9688354-2-5

    I. Burrill, Heather   II. Title.

PS8585.0834R68 2001   jC813'.6   C00-901762-3
PZ7.R719567Ro 2001

For D, N and J,

who taught me most about patience and commitment.

Hi, my name is Rosie. I am seven years old and some of the things I love are ......

Chewing

bones   shoes

teddy bears

anything!

S n i f f i n g

You'll never know what you can discover!

squirrels

cats

C h a s i n g

rabbits

birds

I also LOVE my family. Here is a picture of us:

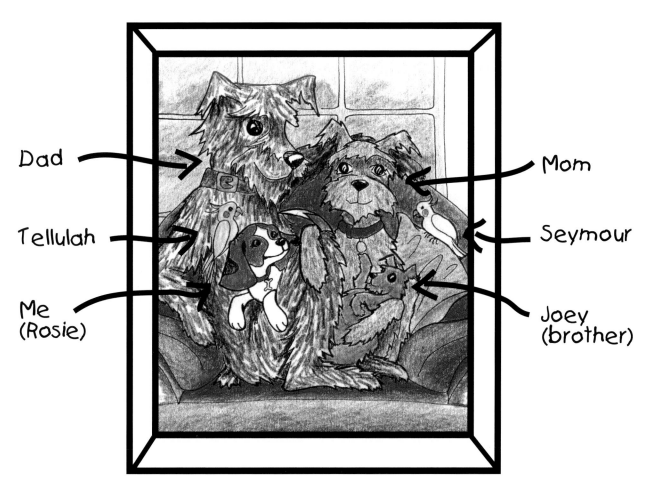

Dad

Tellulah

Me
(Rosie)

Mom

Seymour

Joey
(brother)

You may be wondering why I look different from my family.
It's because I was adopted. That means I was born to a Mom
and Dad who couldn't look after me (I call them birth parents)
so another Mom and Dad (I call them....well, just Mom and
Dad) made me a part of their family.

Some kids are adopted into families, like me........

......and some are born into families, like my brother
Joey who grew inside my Mom.

Mom tells me that all families are special because families are the people who will love you and take care of you no matter where you came from.

When I think about being adopted I sometimes get confused.

So ever since I was little, I have been asking Mom and Dad
LOTS of questions like.......

What was I like when you first brought me home?

After a little while and lots of loving, Mom and Dad said I started

to sleep better

eat better

a
n
d

play all the time!

Are you my **real** parents?

I thought about this when some of the kids at school asked if I knew my **real** parents. That scared me because it made me worry that one day I would have to go live with another family.

When I asked Dad if he was my *real* Dad, he told me to lick his face. "OOOOH" he said, "that tickles. I am definitely *real* and we are definitely a *real* family, **forever!**"

He explained that some people get confused about adoption and call birth parents the *real* parents. Dad says that my birth parents have a special place in my life because I was born to them. He thinks they were brave to let me have a new family even though it probably made them sad.

What were my birth parents like?

We don't know much about them so sometimes
we *imagine* what they look like or how their
voices sound or what their favourite foods are.

Where did I live before?

Sometimes I like to think about the place where I lived before Mom and Dad adopted me. I have a special book with lots of pictures from that place.

I like looking at my book and thinking of my birth family but sometimes I get sad feelings and I wonder if they miss me.

Once I even got *angry* feelings at Mom and Dad for taking me away from my birth parents.

Mom and Dad understand my feelings but have explained that they adopted me *after* my birth parents had decided they could not look after a baby.

They believe my birth parents think about me too and would feel very happy if they knew how much my family loves me.

Do I really belong in my family?

You see, I look different than everyone else in my family and sometimes kids at school don't believe that Joey is my brother.

When I'm feeling sad about being different,
Dad cuddles me and tells me how much he
loves my shiny coat, floppy ears and long tail!

AND Mom says it's good that we are all different.

She also reminds me of how much we are the same.

We all love chasing squirrels, swimming and burying treasures!

After lots of talks with Mom and Dad,
I made an <u>important</u> discovery.

I realized that some of my friends have different families too.

But most importantly, I realized that our families are all the **same**.....

because they **love** us and take good care of us!

Notes For Parents

Rosie's Family highlights several common issues for adoptive families. It was written primarily as a guide for parents to discuss these issues with their children. Please read below for a review of these issues and suggestions for dealing with them. Remember, when discussing adoption with your child, be open; acknowledge your child's thoughts and feelings; give permission for your child to ask questions, particularly about birth parents and be patient.

1. Adoptive families are different.

In order to help your child to feel comfortable within your family, you should stress to your children that differences between people (such as racial, cultural, physical) and differences amongst families (such as birth, adopted, single parent) are good. At the same time similarities between family members and amongst families need to be highlighted.

2. Are adoptive parents the real parents?

A child can receive negative messages about their family from peers who lack an understanding about adoption. In order to confirm to your child your validity as parents, it is essential that you explain to your child that parents are not defined by whom the child was born to, but by whom the child is raised. It is also your responsibility to explain respectfully the role of birth parents in your child's life.

3. Sharing adoption information with your child.

It is your responsibility to talk to your child about being adopted as it is a significant part of her identity. Imagine how distraught your child would be if she found out from someone else. Would she be able to trust you again? What else have you not been honest about? Adopted children often fear betraying their parents by asking them questions about adoption, particularly about birth parents. Your openness about adoption and encouragement to ask questions will help your child gain a better understanding about adoption, which will ultimately help her in resolving many of these confusing issues. A life book which details the child's pre-adoption life and arrival into the adoptive family is a helpful tool for parents to introduce adoption issues to their child and for a child to express questions/feelings about her birth and adoptive families.

4. Sharing birth parent information with your child.

Birth parent information should be presented positively to your child including an acknowledgement of the birth parents' difficulty in making their decision for adoption. This information should be shared as often as it is asked in order to promote a strong feeling of comfort within your child regarding her birth history. In later years, if your child expresses a desire to search for birth family, it is your responsibility to help. She will not be searching for replacement parents, but rather information about her origins to which everyone is entitled.

5. The adjustment period for adopted children into their families.

Expect an adjustment time for yourself and your child following placement, where mutual feelings of attachment may take time to develop (particularly for older children). Older children often display a "honeymoon" phase (impeccable behaviour), followed by a "testing" phase (disagreeable behaviour) before they feel secure enough to attach to new family members. Younger children may display insecurity through poor sleeping and eating, preference for one parent over the other and general irritability. Your expectation for this adjustment period will help you to cope during this difficult time.

6. Child blaming parents for distraught feelings about adoption.

A child may have a strong sense of loss regarding her birth family and consequent feelings of guilt, sadness and anger may be directed towards adoptive parents. When this occurs, you must acknowledge your child's feelings; provide your child with accurate information about her birth history and continue responsible parenting. It is often easier for parents to become permissive towards their emotionally distraught child, but remember, it is the clear rules and boundaries which parents create that promote a sense of security in their child.